The
Bird
WITHDRAWN
FROM STOCK

LAOIS COUNTY LIBRARY
3 0010 00811450 9

The Origami Bird

Lorraine Francis

Illustrated by
Anne O'Hara

POOLBEG
FOR CHILDREN

Published 2001
by Poolbeg Press Ltd
123 Baldoyle Industrial Estate
Dublin 13, Ireland
E-mail: poolbeg@poolbeg.com
www.poolbeg.com

1 3 5 7 9 10 8 6 4 2

A catalogue record for this book is available from the British Library.

ISBN 1 84223 019 0

Cover design by Steven Hope
Illustrations by Anne O'Hara
Typeset by Patricia Hope in Times 16/24
Printed by The Guernsey Press Ltd,
Vale, Guernsey, Channel Islands.

About the Author

Lorraine Francis works as Branch Librarian in Athlone Library. Working in the Public Library service kindled an interest in writing for children. She is married with two sons, the most unbiased critics in the Universe! She has also written *Lulu's Tutu* and *Save Our Sweetshop* for Poolbeg.

In memory of my father, Lionel

“Today we’re going to make things out of paper,” Miss Baker told the class.

The children watched as she took a sheet of green paper and began to fold it. Then she held it up for everyone to see.

“It’s a frog!” cried Anna.

“How did you do that, Miss?” John asked.

“It’s called Origami,” said Miss Baker,

and she wrote the word in big letters on the blackboard. “It means paper-folding,” she explained.

She took a sheet of white paper and began folding again.

"Oh look, it's a bird!" the children cried. "An Origami bird!"

The Origami bird had graceful wings. He looked as if he were about to fly.

Miss Baker made a grasshopper and a blue butterfly. Then the bell rang for break time.

"We'll leave them here," she said, lining them up along the windowsill, and she took the children outside to play.

The sun streamed in through the open window. The Origami bird felt its warmth on his wings. Looking up, he saw birds flying everywhere. He could hear their shrill cries as they swooped and zig-zagged across the sky.

"I will fly too," he said.

"How will you fly?" asked the frog beside him on the windowsill.

"I'm a bird and I have wings," said the Origami bird.

The frog gave a croaking laugh. “I’m a frog,” he said. “Yet I can’t jump or swim in a pond.”

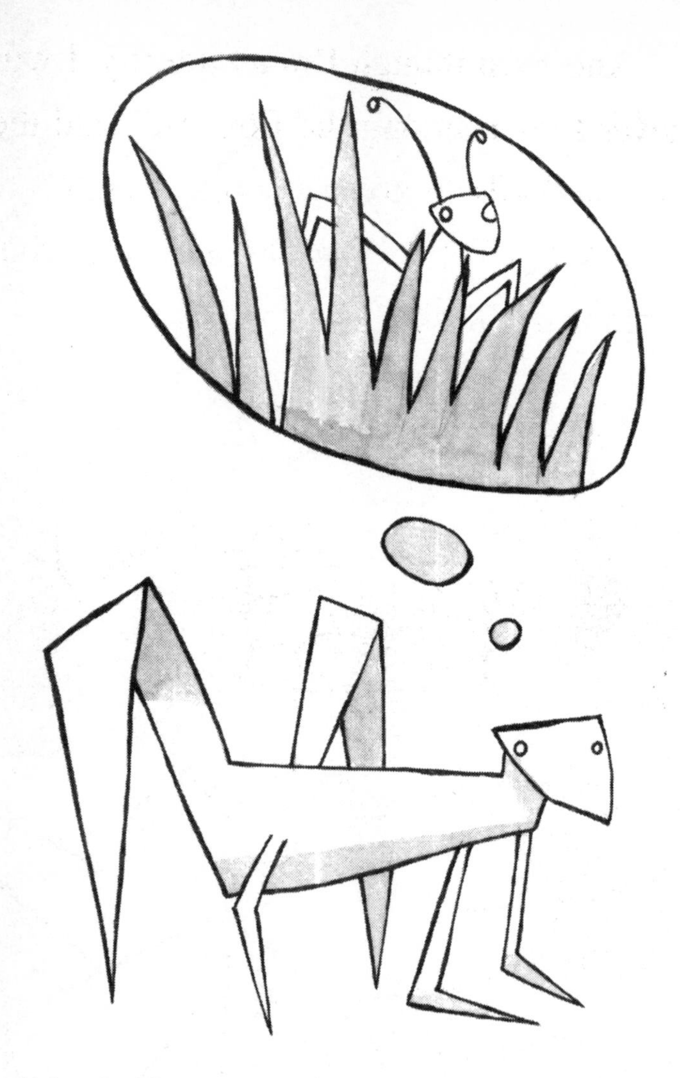

"And I'm a grasshopper," said the grasshopper. "But I can't leap through the long grass."

"And even though I'm a butterfly, I will never flutter among the flowers," said the blue butterfly in a voice soft as a sigh.

"But I will fly," the Origami bird said, looking at the sky.

Just then a big gust of wind whooshed in through the open window. It ran around the classroom, making the pictures on the walls flap and shiver. It rattled the door,

and blew chalk dust everywhere. Then it rushed out through the window again, taking the Origami bird with it.

"I'm flying!" he cried as the wind carried him along.

But then he began to fall: down he drifted, gentle as a feather at first; then he started spinning and tossing, faster and faster . . . Crump! He hit the ground.

One of his wings was bent and twisted. He looked up. The blue sky was miles and miles away.

"Hello!" said a voice, and a wren flew down beside him.

"What kind of bird are you?" the wren asked.

Then a robin with a plump, red breast came bobbing over.

"What kind of bird are you?" he asked, looking at the Origami bird with bright, beady eyes.

"I'm an Origami bird," said the Origami bird shyly.

"An Origami bird!" the wren and the robin twittered.

"Come with us to the big oak tree, Origami bird," the robin said, fluffing up his wings.

"Yes, come along," said the wren. "We build our nests there every Spring."

"But I can't fly," the Origami bird said in a small voice.

"Why can't you fly? Are you hurt?" the wren asked, looking at the crumpled wing.

"No," said the Origami bird sadly. "I can't fly because I'm just a paper bird."

And he told them about the frog, the grasshopper and the butterfly, and how the wind had whirled him out the window.

"We'll take you flying," the robin said, and he took one of the Origami bird's wings gently in his beak. The wren held the other wing and they began to fly.

Up over the school they soared. He could feel the beating of their wings, and the warm wind rushing past.

Far below, the children were playing in the yard; their cries grew fainter as the birds flew higher and higher.

"I'm flying!" the Origami bird said. "At last I'm flying!"

The robin and the wren took him around the big oak tree in the field beside the school. He could hear the swoosh of the wind in the leaves, and the creak of the great branches.

He saw birds building their nests; they flew back and forth with beaks full of twigs and moss.

He heard the chirp and twitter of baby birds waiting to be fed, and the sweet music of a lark singing. He saw a tractor chugging around the field, and lambs skipping along beside their mothers.

In the distance, a river shone like silver in the sun. Then the wren and the robin turned and flew back over the school. The children were lined up in the yard waiting to go back inside.

The birds flew back into the classroom, and landed on the windowsill.

"You were flying!" the butterfly said.

"High in the sky!" said the grasshopper.

"Just like a bird," croaked the frog.

The wren and the robin opened their wings. “We must go now, Origami bird,” they said. “Goodbye, goodbye,” they called as they flew out of the window again.

Miss Baker came back into the classroom with the children. When they were all sitting at their desks again she took the Origami bird down from the windowsill.

"Birds must fly," she said, cutting a long piece of thread from a spool. Then she stood up on a chair and hung him from the ceiling.

"There," she said. "That's where you belong."

The children made birds and butterflies of many colours, and Miss Baker hung them up around the classroom. They floated above their heads like a garden of beautiful flowers.

One day the wren and the robin flew down onto the ledge outside the window.

"Hello, Origami bird," they said, tapping on the glass with their beaks. "Are you happy up there?"

The Origami bird twirled slowly on the end of the thread. Outside he could see birds flying over the big oak tree. It had lost its leaves now that winter was here.

Once he had flown up there with them, and felt the wind on his wings. But now his world was the classroom where he had music when Miss Baker played the piano and the children sang their songs;

each day he heard stories of wisdom and wonder; and when the wind and rain lashed against the window, he was warm and dry inside.

"Yes," he said, "I am happy."

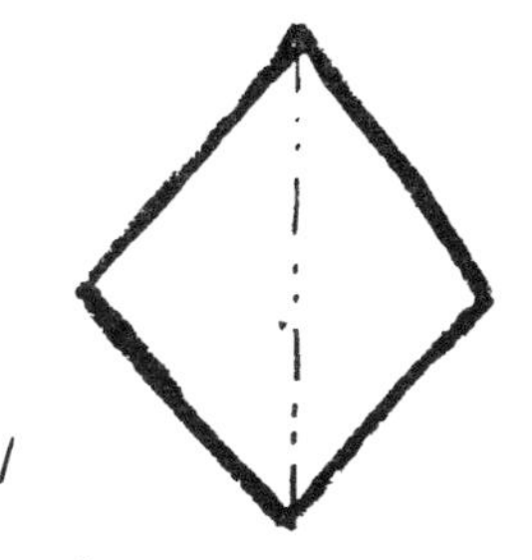

1

Make a crease along a diagonal. Unfold.

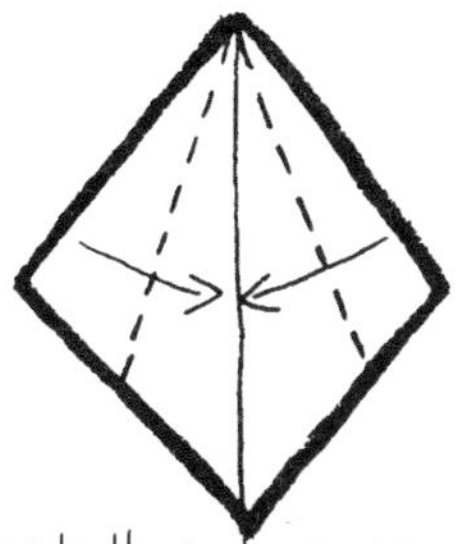

2

Fold two edges to the centre crease. Be careful to make a neat corner at the top.

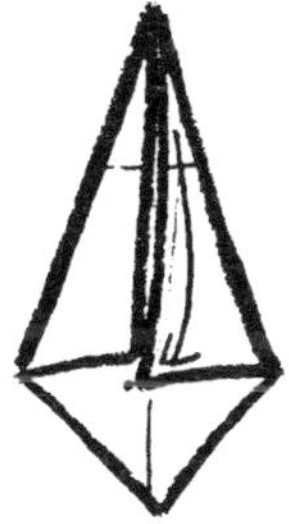

3

Fold dot to dot.

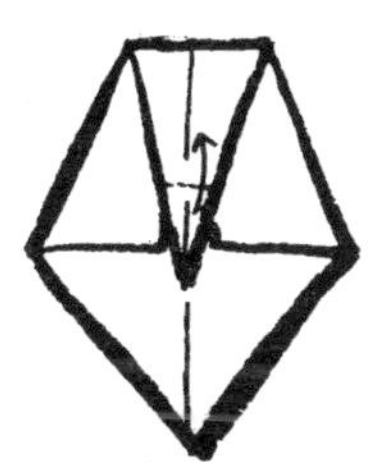

4

Fold the sharp corner back up a little way. The exact distance is unimportant.

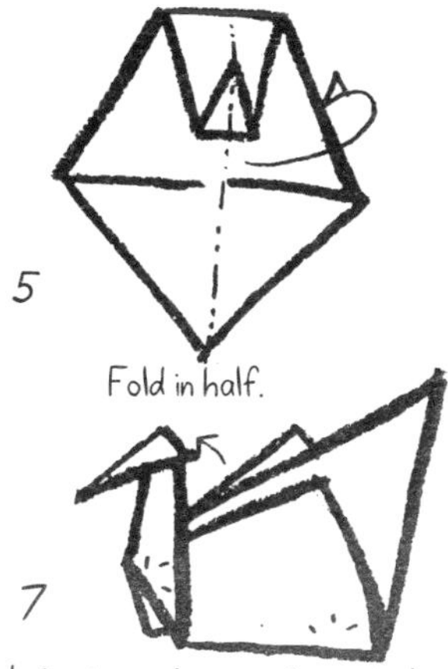

5

Fold in half.

6

Lift the beak away from the neck. Squeeze flat the back of the head to make new creases.

7

Lift the neck away from the body. Squeeze flat the base of the neck to make new creases.

8

The bird is complete.

Why not check with your local library or book shop if you would like to learn more about Origami, the Japanese art of paper-folding?